THE PROFESSOR

BOOK FOUR OF THE CRAFTERS' CLUB SERIES

AN UNOFFICIAL MINECRAFT NOVEL

LOUISE GUY

First edition: 2015.
Printed by Go Direct Publishing Pty Ltd.

Print ISBN: 978-0-9943414-6-4

Edited by Kathy Betts
Cover design by Lana Pecherczyk

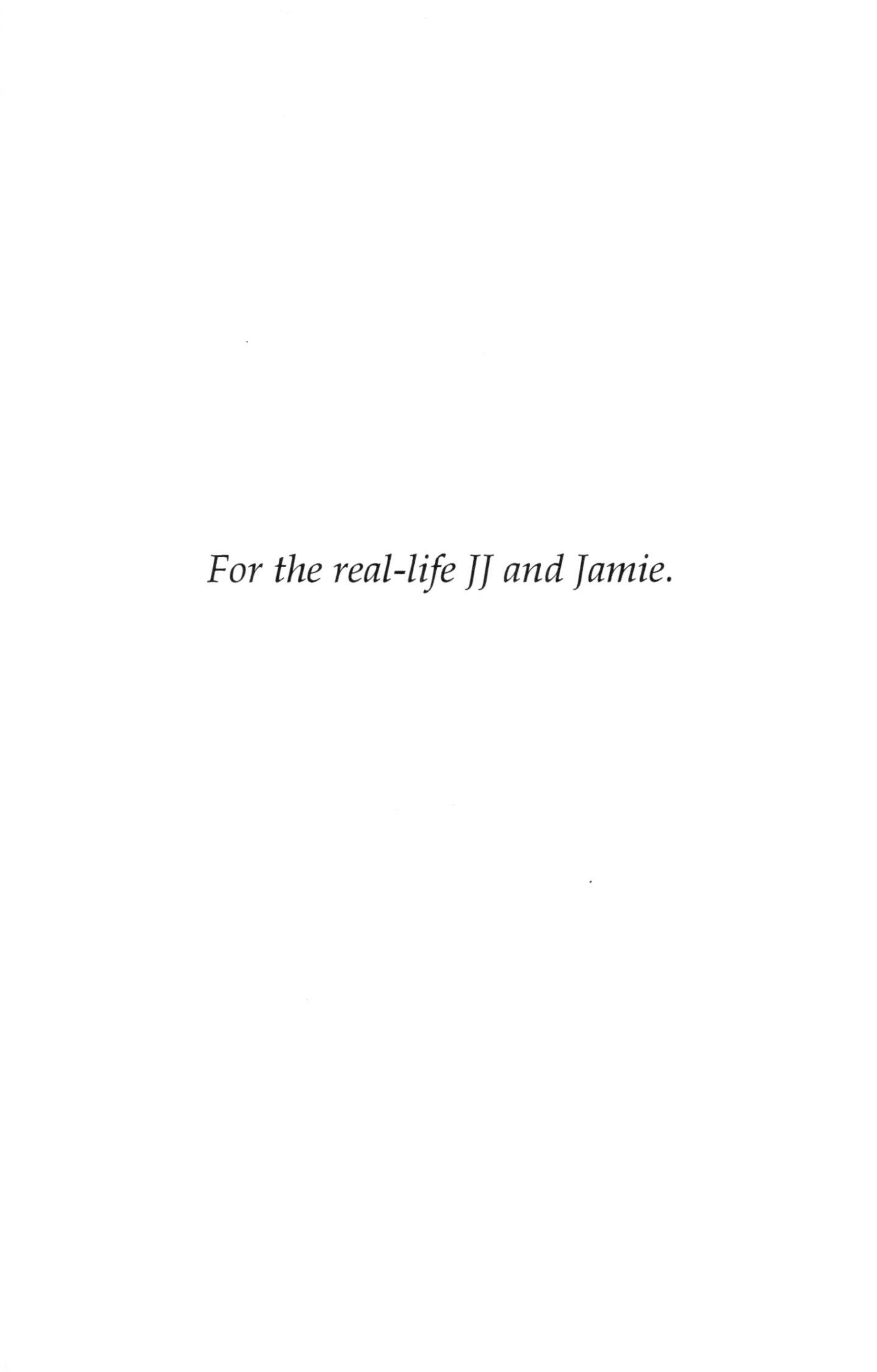

For the real-life JJ and Jamie.

CHAPTER ONE

Annie's Choice

Sprawled out on the front lawn at the boys' house, JJ, Jamie, and Charli waited for Annie to arrive. They'd buzzed with excitement all morning. Which Minecraft map would Annie choose for them to visit? Would it work or would they end up back in the same map as last time?

JJ couldn't imagine Annie would pick anything scary, not after their last adventure. Stuck and unable to return from the Nether had been terrifying.

They'd been forced to duck fireballs, avoid zombie pigmen, and outrun wither skeletons. It was not something he wanted to experience again. It still amazed him that Annie had found the courage to help Jamie rescue himself, Charli, and their villager friend, Toby.

"What time is Annie supposed to be here?" Charli asked.

JJ checked his watch. "Any minute."

"I can't wait to find out which map she's picked," Jamie said.

"My guess is it will be a zoo," Charli said. "She loves animals."

JJ shook his head. "I don't think so. If I know Annie it'll be a map filled with hundreds of cakes."

"Yep, I agree," Jamie said. "Cakes are

all she ever builds. They're her specialty."

"We're about to find out." Charli jumped to her feet as the front door of Annie's house opened and Annie appeared.

Excitement built as Annie crossed the road.

"Hi guys." Annie grinned at the other members of the Crafters' Club. "Ready?"

"We are, are you?" JJ asked. "Did you bring a map?"

Annie pulled a USB stick out of her pocket. "Yep, all ready to load."

"Let's go." Jamie turned and hurried to the house. The others followed.

"So, do you want me to tell you what the map is?" Annie asked.

"No, let it be a surprise," JJ said. "I

just have to convert it for the Xbox. Won't be long." JJ put the USB into his laptop and began the process.

Jamie tapped his fingers on the coffee table. "I can't wait to go back in."

"Me either," Charli said. "Let's hope nothing goes wrong this time."

"Okay, all done." JJ inserted the USB into the Xbox. He clicked through the options and selected the map named Annie's Choice. He grinned at her. "Ready for the big reveal?"

Annie smiled. "Definitely. Open the map, JJ."

The map opened and Annie's selection for their next adventure was revealed.

Jamie jumped up off the couch. "Awesome, this is so awesome. Check it out. Can you believe Annie chose this?" A theme park map had opened on the Xbox.

The other two grinned, their eyes fixed on the screen.

"Let me show you around." Annie picked up a controller and took them on a tour of the map.

"I definitely want to ride the roller coaster," Jamie said.

"I can't wait to see the Ferris wheel," Charli said. "It looks amazing on the screen."

"I wonder if the fairground music will still play when we arrive," Annie said. "It's so festive."

"We thought you would choose a food map," JJ said. "This is heaps better."

"Oh, don't worry," Annie moved CakeGirl1 to another area, "we won't be hungry." She toured the food stalls. All offered a variety of cakes in different colors and sizes.

"As long as we can access them," JJ said. "We should still prepare chests with other food, armor, weapons, and crafting materials."

The other three nodded. They'd learned from their previous adventures that the more prepared they were, the better.

"Should we try out the rides on the Xbox?" Charli asked. "We don't want any surprises when we go in."

"I already have," Annie said. "They all work perfectly. I've even added an emergency stop for the roller coaster."

"Emergency stop?" JJ said. "Why do we need that? Do you think it's too dangerous?"

Annie's cheeks flushed as the others waited for her to answer. She shook her head. "No, it's just…well I wasn't sure if I'd get scared or not. If I do I want to be able to stop the ride and get off."

"Good idea," JJ said. "How do you stop it?"

"By turning off a powered rail. I've placed a button at one halfway through the ride. If you press it the minecart will slow when it travels over the rail and gradually stop."

"So three of us need to stand by the button waiting while one of us is on the ride?" Jamie asked.

Annie nodded. "Yes. When you want to stop just wave your hands like crazy above your head, that can be the signal to push the button."

"I didn't know you knew how to use powered rails," JJ said.

Annie laughed. "It was a good opportunity to learn."

"What else should we check before we go back in?" Jamie asked.

"How to get back out," Charli said. "We'll be in a different map. We should build a portal before we go."

JJ smiled. Everyone was thinking ahead.

"I've made sure to only open the map in creative mode," Annie said. "We might arrive in creative this time."

"Let's hope so but if we don't let's be prepared for survival. Annie, did you want to fill some chests with food?" JJ said. "Charli, why don't you build a new portal? Jamie and I can organize the armor and other inventory."

Annie laughed. "I think you'll find there's enough food."

"Let's put some into the chests anyway," JJ said. "Nothing's gone to plan on our earlier visits so this time let's make sure we're over-prepared."

Silence fell on the family room as the four members of the Crafters' Club got on with their jobs. Ten minutes later they were finished. A portal had been created near the small house Jamie had built at the edge of the theme park. The food and inventory had been placed in chests and stored inside.

"One of the chests is full of obsidian and flint and steel," Jamie said. "We can easily build another portal if we come across any issues."

"Good job." JJ put his controller down on the table and turned to the others. "Ready?"

Three grinning faces nodded.

The four friends raced down the sloping back yard to the dense forest. It was amazing to think they'd discovered the portal only a week ago. The overgrown path was already trampled flat by their frequent trekking back and forth.

Charli led them into the forest. She ducked quickly around branches and fallen logs. Reaching the creek she picked her way across the exposed rocks before racing up the steep bank on the far side. She let out a breath as she rounded the last tree and stepped into the clearing. The bright light of the portal sparkled and danced in the morning sunlight. She turned and grinned at the others. "I was worried it might not be here."

"Me too." Jamie returned her grin. "But it is, so let's go in. I'm dying to ride the roller coaster and try some of the amazing cakes Annie made."

JJ turned to Charli and Annie. "What do you think? Ready?"

Charli's heart rate quickened. "I'm with Jamie, let's go."

"Yes, let's go." Annie laughed at the three surprised faces in front of her. "I know I'm usually the one to chicken out but I've got a good feeling this time. It's going to be fun. Come on."

"Well, if Annie's happy to go in, then I am too," JJ said. "Lead the way, Charli."

Charli approached the portal. She turned to check the others were behind her then squeezed her eyes shut and stepped into its bright, welcoming light.

CHAPTER TWO

The Fun Ends

JJ wondered if the others noticed the difference this time as they were spun and propelled by the portal into the Minecraft world. A rainbow of colors flooded his vision and he spun backward this time, not forward. It stopped abruptly and he found himself standing in the heart of a forest.

He looked down, checking he'd arrived in his Minecraft skin, JJLee45. He had. A lump caught in his throat. Why was he alone and why was he in a forest, not in the theme park?

"Jamie, Charli, Annie," he called, "where are you?" He heard the rustle of leaves and felt a sense of relief as JamieG14, CakeGirl1, and Charli9 appeared.

"Weird." Jamie's blue Minecraft skin made him appear like a warrior rather than a seven-year-old. "I spun differently and saw different colors."

"Me too." Charli's yellow head nodded as she spoke.

"Why are we here?" Annie asked. "This isn't the map I downloaded. Don't tell me we're stuck somewhere we shouldn't be…again."

JJ didn't respond, Annie's fear

reflected his own concerns. He couldn't believe it. Their careful planning was wasted.

"We've gone somewhere different," Charli said. "This doesn't look like the theme park map."

"Hold on, what's that?" Annie glanced around at the trees behind them. "I'm sure I heard something."

Jamie laughed. "Stop worrying, there's nothing there. We're in the Minecraft world. We don't know which map but there's a way to find out. Come on, let's explore."

Charli and Annie followed closely as Jamie pushed his way through the forest.

JJ wished he could be as relaxed as Jamie. He punched at his left arm and his inventory pad appeared. As he'd feared, they were in survival mode with empty inventories. He didn't even have the items he'd crafted in the previous map. The lump in his throat made breathing difficult. This was bad. They'd returned with no inventory, no portal, nothing. Surely the others were worried too? He looked ahead. Jamie had increased his speed. If he wanted to catch up he had no choice but to follow and hope for a miracle.

Jamie came to the edge of the forest and the land spread out in front of him. He stopped and the others caught up.

"This is more like it." Charli looked

out at the familiar landmarks. Hills, lakes, and animals sprawled before them. She pointed to a hill. "Let's go up to the top, see if we recognize anything."

JJ hesitated. Did any of them realize the trouble they were in? Annie would freak out. He'd wait a few minutes and try to think of a solution before saying anything. He followed Charli. He wished he could push his concerns from his mind and enjoy himself as he leaped from block to block. At the top of the hill the view stretched all the way to the horizon.

"Look!" Annie squealed. "Look."

The lump in JJ's throat dissolved. In the distance the Ferris wheel's carriages gleamed in the sunlight and the roller coaster tracks rose high above the landscape. JJ turned to Jamie and grinned. "Phew, I was getting worried."

Jamie nodded. "Me too."

"Really?" JJ asked. "You seemed happy to be here, no matter what."

"I am, but I'd prefer to have our inventory, food, and a way home. Let's go to the park and check the chests and portal are there. You lead Annie, this is your map."

Annie's mouth broke into a wide smile. "Follow me, it's time for some fun." She punched her left arm out twice and sprinted toward the theme park.

JJ followed Jamie and Charli as they raced after Annie. He agreed with her, it was time to have some fun.

❧

By the time they stopped at the theme park entrance JJ's smile was as wide as Annie's. Her excitement was contagious. Music played and the aroma of freshly baked cakes wafted through the air. JJ inhaled. "I love how we can smell in the Minecraft maps."

Jamie laughed. "You weren't so keen when we smelled the cows and their… you know what."

JJ turned up his nose. "No, you're right. I'll restate that. I love how we can smell in this map."

"Let's go check the portal and inventory first," Charli said. "Then we can enjoy ourselves. We need to keep an eye on the sun too, I don't want to be here at nighttime."

JJ checked the sun's location. "It's still high in the sky. We've got plenty of time left."

They followed Charli as she weaved her way around food stalls and rides and made her way to the Ferris wheel. The purple glow from the portal shone behind it. Charli grinned. "Portal's here, and there's the hut Jamie built for the chests."

They walked to the hut and pushed the door open. Chests lined the walls inside. They opened them and filled their inventories with the items.

"We're in survival mode again," Charli said. "Do you think we'll ever arrive in creative?"

JJ shrugged. "I think we need to assume we'll always be in survival. If we're lucky and end up in creative at some point we'll still be prepared."

"Okay, enough standing around," Jamie said.

Charli agreed. "Can we ride the Ferris wheel?"

"No it doesn't move," Jamie said. "We can ride the roller coaster though. Come on." He dashed across the park.

Annie arrived at the roller coaster last. "Only one person can go at a time. JJ, why don't you go first." She pointed to a chest. "Minecarts are in there."

JJ grinned. He placed a minecart on the tracks and jumped in. "Okay, remember the emergency stop signal. If

I wave my arms like this," he waved his hands above his head, "you need to press the lever to turn the powered rail off. Don't do it unless I wave though, I don't want to stop halfway around."

JJ pulled the lever and gripped the sides of the cart. It jumped forward, starting the long climb up the first hill. His heart pounded. He'd only been to one theme park with roller coasters before. He loved them but they still made him nervous.

The cart reached the top of the hill and stopped briefly before it plummeted down the other side. JJ held on as the air whooshed past and the cart vibrated up and over the next hill. He screamed as it rocketed around a tight corner before slowing to climb another rise. He looked down at Jamie, Charli, and Annie as the cart continued its climb. He'd have liked to wave but didn't want them to think he needed the ride stopped. Instead he held on tight, ready for the next rush. He wasn't disappointed. The cart took off down the hill and up over three more. It whizzed around a corner and through a dark tunnel, over another series of hills and then wound itself back toward the start. The cart rumbled to a stop at the end of the track and JJ jumped out as it hit the end block. He punched his cart until it floated in front of him and added it to his inventory. Walking over to join the others, he arrived as Charli climbed into a cart.

"How was it?" Jamie asked. "It looked amazing."

JJ nodded, the smile still plastered on his face. "It was. You've all got to try it." He turned to Annie. He knew she would be nervous. "You'll love it, I promise."

Annie took a deep breath. "Okay, I'll go after Charli."

Charli's cart whizzed around the track. The others could hear her screams of delight as it thundered along, up and down hills then around the curves before coming to a stop. She jumped out, collected her cart, and raced back over to the group. "That was amazing. I could see for miles from the top of the first hill. I'm sure I saw horses in the distance," she said. "Did you see them, JJ?"

JJ shook his head. "I didn't even think to look at the view. I was too busy holding onto the cart."

"I thought I could see a person too but the cart dropped so quickly down the hill. It might have been an animal or tree, I'm not sure."

"My turn." Annie climbed into the minecart. Jamie pushed the lever and they watched as her cart moved off.

"Did you see that?" Charli pointed to the far side of the ride. "A dog just ran behind the trees."

JJ shook his head. "I didn't see anything, are you sure?"

"I saw it," Jamie said. "It was a wolf, not a dog."

"No, it had a red collar. It's a wolf

that's been tamed and turned into a dog," Charli said. "I hope we see it again. I'd like to pat it, see if its coat feels like fur." She turned her attention back to the roller coaster. "Can you believe Annie's on this? She's usually scared of everything."

"She used to be," Jamie said. "I think our trip to the Nether brought out a whole new Annie. She's more confident. I thought she'd be the one who'd stop us coming through the portal, not the one who'd choose the map."

"There she goes." JJ watched the cart whiz down the first hill and up the next.

"She's waving at us," Jamie said. "You didn't even bother JJ, you were too scared to let go."

"No I wasn't. I was afraid you'd think

I wanted the ride stopped." Annie's arms waved frantically above her head. "She's still waving, something's wrong."

JJ looked along the track to where the cart headed. His eyes widened when he saw the problem. He pushed past Jamie and brought his hand down on the emergency stop button.

The track was on fire.

CHAPTER THREE

The Weird Professor

JJ held his breath as Annie's cart continued to fly along the track. It hurtled down a hill and across a flat section toward the powered rail.

Annie screamed as the cart careened past them. It crossed the powered rail and started to slow, but didn't stop. The cart continued toward the fire.

"It didn't work," Charli said. "She had too much speed coming down the hill. Annie's going to be burned. What do we do? JJ, Jamie, we need to do something."

JJ raced to a curve in the track and punched at the rails. They broke. It was the last corner before the cart would move into the home stretch which now raged with flames and sparks. He moved back as the cart approached the curve. He could see Annie's white, panicked face.

JJ closed his eyes, he couldn't watch. He heard a cry, followed by a cheer and forced one eye open. The cart had stopped.

"Are you okay?" JJ ran over and wrapped Annie in his arms. She wasn't okay. Tears welled in her green eyes and her body shook all over.

Charli and Jamie arrived next to them, concern etched on both their faces.

"The fire's getting bigger," Jamie said. "Should we do something?"

"I think we should go to the portal and leave," Charli said.

"Yes, good idea. Come on Annie, let's get you home." JJ ushered Annie toward the Ferris wheel and portal. Charli followed.

"Wait a minute," Jamie called, "there's someone else here."

JJ stopped. Someone else? There couldn't be anyone else. "What do you mean?"

"Look." Jamie pointed to the section of the roller coaster that was on fire. They could no longer see flames but smoke rose from the end of the track. "It's steam," Jamie said, "not smoke.

Someone's throwing water on the fire. They're putting it out."

ꟹ

Jamie was right. A figure moved around the coaster track where the fire was almost extinguished.

"I think we should go," Annie said.

"Don't you want to find out who it is?" Jamie asked. "I do."

"So do I," Charli said. "He's put out the fire so he must be a good guy."

"Not if he started it," Annie said.

Charli turned to JJ. "What do you think? Should we go and see who he is?"

They'd had another near miss with Annie on the roller coaster. The safest thing to do now was to leave the Minecraft world and go home. "Why don't we go out and come back in on the Xbox," he said. "See who he is without putting ourselves at risk."

"Good idea," Annie agreed.

"We won't be able to talk to him from the Xbox," Jamie said. "Why don't you and Annie go? Charli and I will stay and meet him. We'll say hi and then come straight back out, won't we, Charli?"

Charli nodded.

"No, we should stick together," JJ said. "What if the portal takes us somewhere else? We assume it will take us home but we don't know for sure."

"I think our decision's been made for us," Annie said.

The figure moved in their direction.

Jamie spoke in a whisper. "He looks really weird."

JJ agreed. Sporting a big white coat, red eyes, and green hair, he looked strange.

"Hello there." The man approached the group. "Nice to meet you. Are you all okay?" He stared at Annie. "You were lucky on the coaster." He turned to JJ. "Nice save."

"Thanks," JJ said. "So who are you? Do you live here?"

The man laughed. "They call me The Professor. Now, lots to do, lots to do, must get on." He turned and walked away, leaving the group staring after him.

"He's bizarre," Charli said. "Hold on, where did he go? He disappeared, did you see that?"

Charli was right, the professor had vanished. "I've got no idea," JJ said. "Unusual things are happening. It's different from any map I've played."

"Let's not worry about him," Annie said. "I want to go. Now."

JJ agreed. "Let's go, we'll talk about it when we get home. Come on, Annie."

He grasped Annie's arm and stepped into the purple light. The tug of the portal propelled him forward. Please let this portal take us home, he thought. They'd tested their luck one time too many going into the Minecraft world.

JJ didn't care what the others said. It was too dangerous. This was definitely going to be their last adventure.

❧

"Phew." JJ let go of Annie's arm as they stepped onto the soft grass. "At least the portal brought us home and not to the Nether or somewhere else."

Annie gave a shaky smile. "I think I've had enough. No more adventures."

JJ nodded. "I agree. We're going to run out of luck and one of us might get hurt. We'll tell Jamie and Charli when they come out."

"Where are they?" Annie asked. "They should be here by now."

JJ fixed his gaze on the portal. Jamie had probably made a last minute decision to explore or to try to find the professor. His thoughts were interrupted as the purple light flashed and Jamie stepped out.

He grinned. "Home again. Awesome, I thought we might be unlucky and end up back in the Nether."

JJ laughed. "That's what I thought. Where's Charli?"

Jamie looked around. "She was right behind me, she'll be here any second."

A few minutes passed while they waited for her.

"Where is she?" Annie asked. "Something's happened, she wouldn't explore on her own."

"Annie's right," Jamie said. "I suggested we go and find the professor and she said no. She practically pushed me into the portal."

"Okay," JJ said. "Who wants to come with me?" There was no choice, they had to go back and find Charli.

Annie shook her head.

"I'll come," Jamie said. "Will you be okay here by yourself, Annie?"

"No, and neither of you are going back in either."

"What do you mean?" Jamie said. "Of course we are, we have to."

"No we don't. Let's go back to your house. If we find Charli she'll know we're on the Xbox because we won't be able to talk to her. It worked when we wanted to find Toby. Let's do it again," Annie said.

"She's right," JJ said. "It makes sense to go home."

"You and Annie go home, I'll go

back through the portal," Jamie said. "We won't be able to help Charli from the Xbox. We need to be inside the map to help. You couldn't help when the villager poisoned me and we couldn't help Toby when he was lost in the Nether. I'll go in and you two come and find me. You can lead me to Charli if there's a problem and I can't find her myself."

JJ thought for a moment. Jamie was right. At least one of them needed to be in the map. "Okay, go back to the theme park. Annie and I will run home and join you from the Xbox."

Jamie grinned.

"But, Jamie," JJ said, "you are to come straight out once we've found Charli, earlier if I tell you to. Okay?"

Jamie nodded and stepped into the glowing purple light.

CHAPTER FOUR

Charli's in Trouble

At the exact moment Charli put one foot into the portal something wrenched her back. She collapsed on the ground. The sun blinded her, adding to her confusion. What was going on?

An evil laugh rang out. She struggled to her feet, raising her hand to block the sun. The knot in her stomach tightened as the laughter got louder. The professor stood in front of her, his fiery eyes boring into hers.

"What are you doing?" Charli's knees shook. "And what's so funny?"

The professor stopped laughing. "No talking." He grabbed her shirt. "You're coming with me."

Charli struggled as the professor dragged her toward the theme park exit.

He stopped and shook her. "Stop. You're making this far too hard."

"Tell me what you're doing and where you're taking me," she said.

"I said be quiet," the professor shouted. He reached into his jacket and pulled out a small jar containing a red liquid. He removed the lid and threw the contents into her eyes.

Charli's legs crumpled and a strange sensation flooded over her as she fell.

Part of her brain told her to be frightened yet her entire body relaxed, her cheeks straining from the enormous smile on her face.

"Very good," the professor said. "Life will be much easier for us both. Now, time to try out an invention or two."

Charli couldn't talk, her mouth only wanted to smile. A giggle rose in the back of her throat. She wished she could stop the potion but she had no control over her body. The professor stood beside her. He didn't touch her but Charli knew she was moving. She twisted her head back and forth. What was happening? She looked to her feet. The ground was a long way down. Was she flying? No, it had to be her imagination. Heat surrounded her and she lay back. It was so lovely and warm. She closed her eyes.

"Get up."

Charli forced her eyes open. She put her hands down, sand scrunched between her fingers. The professor was above her, his face stony. She tried to stand but her legs wobbled. She no longer felt relaxed or calm. Trying again, she dragged herself up and looked around. She stood on an island, a very small island, completely surrounded by lava. Charli wasn't sure which was more frightening, her location or her crazy-eyed companion.

JamieG14 arrived back in the Minecraft map. He didn't waste any time. He raced out of the thick forest and continued on, past lakes and hills. Cows grazed in the shadow of a mountain making him think of his cow. Bessie, as JJ had named her. How were she and her calf doing? He shook himself, he needed to think about Charli.

Jamie reached the theme park and stopped to eat two pork chops. He wanted to keep his hunger bar full. Thank goodness they'd filled the chests with food and other inventory. Music greeted him as he walked through the entrance. He moved in the direction of the portal but he couldn't see Charli. He reached the portal as JJLee45 and CakeGirl1 arrived.

JJLee45 and CakeGirl1 walked off in different directions. They'd begun their search for Charli. Jamie decided to search the roller coaster area. Perhaps the professor had seen her.

Jamie searched the area around the roller coaster. The smell of burned track lingered. He reached a tall wall, the park's boundary, before he turned back.

As he walked back to the portal a gale of wind and dust blew over him. He closed his eyes and coughed. When he opened them, JJLee45 stood in front of him, his sword pointed at the wall. Jamie wished he could talk.

JJ gestured to the wall again and then pointed his sword in the other direction. When JJLee45 walked to the theme park exit, Jamie followed.

They went out through the park

gates. Annie waited for them along the side wall of the theme park. Jamie smiled. She looked awesome. The diamond sword and diamond armor she wore made her look fierce. A warrior-like figure in contrast with her usual cake-girl appearance. Behind Annie sheep grazed next to a water-filled lake. She jumped up and down, her sword pointing away from the theme park.

Jamie turned to look. A lava lake stretched out before him, bigger than any he'd seen in Minecraft. He took a step back and wiped his forehead. His shirt would soon be soaked if sweat kept pouring down his back. Annie and JJ moved close to the edge of the lava, but he couldn't. They were so close it amazed him they didn't catch on fire. Annie continued to jump up and down.

Jamie squinted. She was pointing to an island. A figure moved from one side of the island to the other. He rubbed his eyes and looked again. It was Charli.

JJ stared at the television screen. They'd found Charli.

"Why doesn't Jamie save her?" Annie asked. "He's got a bucket and there's a lake right beside him. He knows throwing water on the lava will turn it to obsidian or cobblestone."

"I'm not sure," JJ said. "Perhaps he needs a reminder." JJ moved JJLee45 over to the lake and opened his inventory, ready to select a bucket. He groaned. "Great. It's done that thing again."

"Which thing?" Annie asked.

"The one where our inventory disappears. We can't help from here, exactly like Jamie predicted."

"Don't worry, I think he's worked it out already."

Jamie had taken a bucket from his inventory and now filled it with water from the lake. They watched as he threw the water at the lava. It fell short, landing on the grass.

"Oh no," Annie said. "What can he do now?"

Jamie went back to the lake and walked into it.

"He's cooling himself down," JJ said.

"Hopefully he can get closer this time."

Jamie refilled the bucket and moved next to the lava.

JJ grinned at Annie. "He's heaps closer, cooling himself down worked."

This time the water landed on the lava. But instead of the lava turning to obsidian, the water sizzled, hissed and disappeared.

"What happened?" Annie asked. "Why didn't it work?"

JJ shook his head. "I don't know, it doesn't make sense. He's going to try again, watch."

Jamie tried three more times to throw water on the lava but each time the result was the same. He stopped after the fourth bucket and paced.

"He's trying to think of an idea," JJ said. "The sun's about to set, he needs to get out of there."

"So does Charli," Annie said.

"She'll be okay where she is, no mob is going to try and cross a lava lake. Let's get Jamie home." JJ moved his character next to Jamie and motioned for him to follow. Jamie understood he needed to come out. They watched as he followed JJLee45 to the portal, stepped through, and disappeared.

"Okay, let's hurry back to the forest," Annie said. "Jamie will be wondering where we are."

JJ put his controller on the coffee table and stood. He was about to follow Annie when a movement on the screen caught his eye. "Annie, wait."

Annie stopped at the doorway and turned around. She moved closer and gasped.

The professor, with his white coat and crazy green hair, flew across the lava to Charli's island.

Jamie burst into the family room. "I thought you'd meet me in the forest," he said. "What are you doing?"

"Charli's in trouble," JJ said. "We're trying to work out how to rescue her."

"I know, I saw her on the island. I tried to throw water on the lava but it turned to steam and disappeared. Something's gone wrong. Can we do anything from here?"

"I don't think so. We've got a bigger problem than the lava. Look." JJ motioned to the screen. The professor walked back and forth on the island next to Charli.

"What's he doing?" Jamie asked.

"We don't know," JJ said. "He flew across the lava."

"So he's in creative?" Jamie said.

"I guess so. Let's watch and see what he does."

They sat and watched as the professor stopped occasionally to throw something at Charli.

"What's he throwing on her from those bottles?" Annie asked.

"Potions?" Jamie suggested. "Let's hope he's not trying to poison her like the villager did to me."

JJ shook his head. "I can't imagine why he would go to so much effort. Putting her on an island surrounded by lava just so he can poison her? No, I think he's up to something else."

"Do you think he's put some kind of potion on the lava, so throwing water on it won't work?" Jamie asked.

JJ wasn't sure. Could the professor really make a potion to do that?

"He's flying again," Annie said.

The professor flew away from Charli, across the lava, and back to the theme park.

"The sun's about to set. He's leaving her on the island by herself," Jamie said.

"Let's hope her inventory works," JJ said. "She's smart and the lava will work in her favor at nighttime. Mobs aren't going to cross over it. I'd like to know where he's going."

"To our portal," Jamie said.

The professor landed on the grass in front of the portal. He glanced around, then stepped into the purple light.

Charli looked out across the lava. Was the professor coming back? He wanted her to try out his experiments. He hadn't hurt her, not yet anyway. He'd thrown one potion on her from a strange blue and green soda can that had made her see spiders, hundreds of them. They weren't the usual Minecraft spiders though. There were no glowing eyes, no attacks. These spiders were pink with white eyes that reminded Charli of marshmallows. They sang and tap-danced. It was incredible, Charli had never seen anything like it. She wanted to watch them some more but the spiders disappeared and she was faced once again with the professor.

She only had time to look at him before he threw another potion on her. This time different foods floated toward her. She could see them, smell them, even taste them when they were close enough. She wasn't sure if she was allowed to eat them but she couldn't stop herself, it was all so delicious. Like the spiders, the food disappeared and the professor stood before her.

He was preparing a green potion

when he yelped. "Oh no, the sun, the sun." He rose into the sky and flew toward the theme park.

Charli peered around. The sun was going down. She assumed she would be safe with the lava around her. She tapped her left arm and her inventory pad appeared. Switching it on, a message appeared across the screen. 'Sorry my dear, food is the only inventory you may have while I conduct my experiments. Regards, The Professor.' Charli groaned and sat back on the sand. She had nothing to use to escape or protect herself. There was nothing on the island but sand.

Throwing a cake at the professor, or at a mob, was hardly going to help.

❧

"Quick, we need to see who comes out of the portal." JJ flung his controller onto the coffee table and ran out of the room. "Whoever it is will be the one keeping Charli prisoner."

The others followed as JJ dashed through the house, out the back door and down to the forest. They crossed the creek, hurrying up the steep bank

JJ stopped when he reached the top. He turned to the others and put a finger to his lips. Something rustled in the bushes nearby.

They moved behind a large tree as the sound came closer.

A grey dog appeared. Its tongue hung

toward the ground and his tail wagged furiously.

JJ exhaled. "It's only a dog. Let's go to the clearing and see if there's any sign of someone having been there."

"Hold on," Jamie said. "He looks like the wolf Charli and I saw near the roller coaster."

"He's a dog, not a wolf," Annie said.

"Are you sure?" Jamie asked. "Look at his eyes, they're yellow, just like a wolf's. Although he does have a red collar, Charli noticed that when we saw him. Maybe he came out of the map with the professor."

The dog walked to JJ and sat at his feet. JJ patted its head. "I think he's just a regular dog and our imaginations are running wild. Come on, let's check the portal." He continued to the clearing. There was no sign of anyone else.

"We must have missed him," Annie said. "But we definitely saw the professor use this portal."

"He might have ended up in the Nether," Jamie said. "He'd only come out to the real world if he was a real person."

"Yes," JJ said, "and unless we find him out here, we're never going to know who he is."

"What should we do?" Annie asked. "Do we wait for him to come back or do we go in and try to save Charli?"

JJ thought about his answer. How would they save Charli? That was the real question.

Jamie's voice broke into his thoughts.

"If the professor put a potion on the lava to stop us turning it to obsidian, we need to be smarter. We have to find a way to cross it."

JJ nodded. "How?"

Jamie thought for a moment. "A potion of fire resistance. We make it, drink it, and swim across the lava to the island. We'll have to make enough to give Charli some, then we all swim back. Simple."

"Is it simple to make?" Annie asked.

"Yes, if you have everything you need to make the potion," JJ said. "Which includes a brewing stand."

"The professor is making potions somehow. Perhaps he's got all the equipment. Let's go in and search the theme park, try to find it," Jamie said.

"Okay," Annie said. "We know doing things on the Xbox won't work."

Annie's agreement to go back in surprised JJ. "Really?"

Annie took a deep breath and nodded. "Charli will be scared. She needs to know we're trying to save her."

Jamie grinned. "Going to the Nether changed you. You're not a scaredy-cat anymore."

Annie's smile wobbled. "I'm not sure if I've changed, my legs are like jelly."

JJ put an arm around her shoulders. "Don't worry, so are mine." With his arm still around her they walked through the clearing and into the sparkling light of the portal.

CHAPTER FIVE

Potions

JJ, Jamie, and Annie raced from the forest to the theme park. When they arrived in the map JJ was relieved to find it was daytime. Nighttime, and the mobs that came with it, were not something he wanted to deal with right now. They reached the entrance and stopped.

"Okay," JJ said. "Let's split up. Annie, you search the area at the front of the park, I'll search the middle. Jamie you go to the back, yell if you find anything."

The other two nodded and moved to their areas. JJ hoped he might be lucky and stumble across something useful. He searched the food stands first. There were plenty of chests but his disappointment grew with each one he opened. Cakes and more cakes. That's all they contained. He was about to give up when he heard a yell. It was Jamie.

His heart thumped as he rushed over. Please let Jamie have found something, he thought. Anything to make this easier.

"Look." Jamie stood next to a hut. "I think I've found it."

Annie joined the boys. "What is it?"

"Some kind of laboratory," Jamie said. "Come and look, it's full of potions and all sorts of weird stuff."

They moved inside. A brewing stand stood against one wall, chests and glass bottles lined another. A third wall was covered in paintings. They were all of unicorns.

"Weird," JJ said. "You don't get unicorns in Xbox maps."

"Maybe he just likes them," Annie said. "I know I do."

Jamie's attention was fixed on the brewing stand and chests, not the unicorns. "This is so awesome."

JJ agreed. "We need to be quick, the professor might come back any minute. Who knows what he'll do to us."

"Okay," Annie said, "so how do we make a fire resistance potion?"

Charli was relieved when the sun rose. It hadn't been too bad. Being surrounded by lava was useful. She'd seen things moving on the land near the theme park but wasn't sure what they were. Creepers, zombies, and endermen, probably. She was convinced she'd heard horses whinnying.

The lava prevented the mobs from coming to the island which was good but it stopped her from leaving, too. She sighed. Had the others thought up a plan to save her? Whatever they were doing, she wished they would hurry. Being thrown into boiling lava was not how she wanted to start, or end, her day.

❧

The brewing stand was the only equipment required to make a potion of fire resistance. JJ could hardly believe their luck. Things were going their way at last. All they needed now was a bottle of water, a nether wart, and magma cream.

"Water and magma cream are in here." Annie opened another chest. "I can't find a nether wart though."

JJ and Jamie opened the remaining chests. They contained a wide variety of materials but no nether warts. "We're going to have to find some ourselves," Jamie said.

"Is that hard?" Annie asked.

JJ and Jamie exchanged a look.

"I'll go," Jamie said, not answering Annie's question.

"Go where?" Annie's eyes narrowed.

"The Nether."

The color drained from her face. "Of course, the Nether. They were growing in the fortress, I remember seeing them."

JJ nodded. "So do I. But we're in a different map. You won't end up in the same Nether. You'll have to start again, find a new fortress. It's too dangerous to go alone, I should come with you, or we should all go."

"No," Jamie said. "You need to stay here and check that Charli's okay. What if the professor moves her? We need to know exactly what he's doing. I'll be fine. If I'm lucky it won't take long. I'll get the nether wart and come straight back out."

As much as he didn't want Jamie going to the Nether alone, JJ knew his brother was right. "You'll need to build a new portal, you realize that don't you?"

Jamie nodded. "Yep, I know exactly what to do. Why don't you two hide in case the professor comes back? Somewhere you can watch from but won't get caught."

Annie shook her head. "I can't believe we're doing this again."

Jamie laughed. "Don't be silly, this is the fun bit. I've got plenty of inventory, hopefully it still exists when I get to the Nether. If it doesn't I'll be extra careful, get the warts and come back. If I haven't returned by the time the sun sets go out and search for me on the Xbox."

"But be careful, okay?" JJ said.

Jamie grinned. "I'm always careful. Now you two hide, I'll go outside the theme park to make the new portal."

Jamie's confidence evaporated as he lay the obsidian for the new portal. He thought back to their last journey into the Nether. Being attacked by ghasts and chased by wither skeletons hadn't been fun. He hoped he would arrive with inventory this time and that the portal would stay intact. Then all he'd need to worry about was getting the nether warts.

Jamie lit the portal with flint and steel and jumped back as a whoosh of purple filled the inside. He took a deep breath and before he could change his mind, stepped inside.

❧

JJ and Annie crouched behind the counter of one of the sideshow games. It was unlikely the professor would find them here.

"Do you think Jamie will be okay?" Annie asked.

"I hope so," JJ said. "I really don't want to go back into the Nether to save him."

"Me either, I never want to go there again."

They waited, the happy theme park music at odds with how they felt. They crouched down further as the sound of a cheerful whistle grew louder. JJ peeked around the side of the counter and watched the professor walk into the lab.

"Do you think he's going to make more potions?" Annie asked.

"He might, he's trying things out on Charli." JJ hoped the professor wasn't going to hurt her.

They remained hidden. Jars clanged and sizzling noises erupted from the professor's lab.

JJ wished time would hurry up. Waiting was torture. It gave him far too much time to think of all the bad things that could happen. Their nice day out at the theme park had turned into a nightmare.

❧

Charli's eyes strained as she tried to work out what was happening near the theme park. She thought she could see a portal. But that was crazy. Their portal was on the other side of the Ferris wheel and she couldn't see that from here.

She opened her inventory and selected a cake. At least she could eat. The frosting melted and dripped on the sand. She sighed, the cake looked exactly how she felt, overheated. She ate, glad she didn't have to ration the food. If she ever got out of here she'd need to thank Annie.

Charli swallowed her mouthful and licked her lips. She considered eating another cake when a tap on the shoulder made her jump. Her heart pounded as she turned. Please be JJ, Jamie, or Annie. It wasn't.

"Morning my dear, I see you survived the night."

Charli took a step back.

"So today I have something special for you." The professor smiled. "You are very useful. I've needed someone to test my potions for a long time."

"Why don't you try them yourself?" Charli asked.

The professor laughed. "Excellent question." He held up his thumb and finger a small distance apart. "There is a very slight chance the potion might not do what I think it will. I'd hate to be the guinea pig and die a painful death by mistake. I haven't worked out if we can respawn, or if we would die in both the Minecraft map and the real world."

Charli shivered. Die in the real world? So he was a real person. How had he found his way into the Minecraft map?

The professor cackled. "Have you worked out my plan yet?"

Charli didn't respond.

"Yes, my dear girl, I intend to find out if we can respawn. I want to try two or three more potions on you first. Then, for the grand finale, I'll get you to jump into the lava. I'll push you if you need a hand and we can see what happens. You'll most certainly die but the question is, will you die in the real world as well?"

Charli's throat constricted. She gulped for air. He was going to kill her.

"Oh, don't look so panicked my dear. I'm running out of time to test my theory today. Look," he pointed to the horizon, "the sun's sinking, we'll need to leave it until tomorrow. For now, drink this potion. I want you nice and relaxed."

Charli pressed her lips together and refused.

The professor smirked. "Do you think I'm silly? My potions are also splash potions." He threw the potion into Charli's face, laughing at her stunned reaction. "Enjoy, I'll be back tomorrow. We can see how you like swimming in lava."

Charli smiled and waved to the professor as he flew off toward the theme park. For goodness sake, she shouldn't be waving at him, he was going to kill her. The potion was too strong. She groaned and sat back on the sand. She needed the effects to wear off before she could even begin to think of an escape plan.

JJ and Annie watched as the professor flew back from the island.

"We'd better hide again," JJ said. They'd moved out from behind the sideshow counter when the professor had flown across to Charli's island. "Although the sun's setting so he might go straight back out. He seems to be scared of the nighttime, afraid of mobs probably."

"You'd think he would test some of

his potions on them," Annie said.

"Quick, duck behind here." JJ pulled Annie behind a cake stand. "He can't see us here but we can see the portal through the cracks."

A few moments passed before they heard the professor's familiar whistle. The sun set as he landed in front of the portal.

"Look, he's got the wolf-dog with him," Annie said.

The grey dog sniffed around the base of the portal. Was it really the same animal they'd seen in the forest? Had the professor brought a real dog with him into the Minecraft map or was he a Minecraft wolf the professor had tamed, turned into a dog, and taken out to the real world?

The professor yelped. A bright light flashed as a creeper exploded nearby. Not waiting another second, he ran straight into the purple light. The dog followed.

JJ jumped to his feet. "They've gone. We need full diamond armor and diamond swords. Quick, open your inventory."

Annie followed JJ's instruction and in a few seconds they were both equipped with full diamond protection.

"Hopefully we won't need it," JJ said. "But it's better to be safe than sorry."

Annie nodded, the chatter of her teeth almost drowned out by the theme park music.

"Come on," JJ said. "Let's wait near the portal Jamie created, he should be back soon."

They weaved their way out of the theme park to Jamie's portal. Annie jumped and grabbed hold of JJ's arm.

"What?"

"Listen," Annie whispered.

JJ strained to hear above the music. Then he heard it. It sounded like a wild animal, like jaws that crunched on bone. JJ pulled Annie behind him. "Stay behind me and whatever you do, don't look at it." He knew that sound. They hadn't encountered one in the Minecraft world yet, he'd hoped they never would.

Annie gasped as the creature's long black limbs came into view.

JJ crouched, pulling Annie down next to him. They could be lucky, the enderman might not see them. Annie trembled, her diamond armor rattled against her chest. She lifted her head to look.

"No, Annie, don't look at it."

But it was too late.

JJ leaped up. He held his diamond sword out in front of him as the enderman moved closer. There was no choice but to attack. "Don't look anywhere but at its legs. We need to kill it."

Annie nodded and held her diamond sword out.

The enderman approached, the crunching noise had stopped. It was now in attack mode and its screams were terrifying.

JJ took four strides toward the creature and chopped at the end of its legs. It screeched and hissed as he swung his sword. He kept his gaze fixed on the bottom of its legs. He hoped if he attacked the enderman's legs it wouldn't teleport and attack from a different direction. He swung again and again, trying to block out the horrible noises it made. All went quiet. JJ exhaled. The enderman was dead. An enderpearl floated where it once stood. JJ collected it and put it in his inventory.

Expecting Annie to be hiding, JJ turned to find her battling another enderman. JJ raced to her, the noise of the enderman increasing as he got closer. As he reached them, Annie, with a powerful swing of her sword, killed it. She collected two enderpearls that floated where the creature had been, and hurried over to him.

She must have been so scared, he should never have put her in this position. How would he make it up to her? "I'm so sorry Annie. I was meant to protect you, I've let you down."

"Don't be silly." Annie's face glowed with excitement. "You can't kill two at once. I can't believe I killed an enderman." She didn't seem frightened or even rattled.

"I'm not sure you're supposed to feel so good about it," JJ said.

Annie shrugged. "Well I do. I can defend myself in here, it's awesome."

"You're awesome." JJ smiled, he couldn't wait to tell Jamie and Charli. "The sun's beginning to rise," he said.

Annie looked to the horizon where JJ pointed and let out a delighted squeal.

"Better still, look, Jamie's back."

JJ and Annie ran to meet Jamie.

Annie hugged him. "Are you okay?"

"Don't ask," Jamie put his diamond sword back into his inventory. "The main thing is I got some nether warts. I'll tell you the rest when we get home. Although," he looked them up and down, "the fact you're both in full diamond armor makes me think you've had your own adventure."

JJ grinned. "You could say that. Annie killed an enderman."

Jamie turned to Annie, his face flushed with excitement. "No way. You did what?"

"It was no big deal, JJ killed one too," she said. "We didn't have much choice."

"No big deal? My trip to the Nether was easy compared to that. Tell me what happened."

JJ shook his head. "We'll fill you in later. Let's get this potion made before the professor comes back. He left through the portal when nighttime fell. The sun's just risen so hopefully we've got some time before he returns."

They raced to the lab, flung the door open and moved inside.

"How many warts did you get?" JJ asked.

"Two, that's all I could find. Do you think it will be enough? We can make three potions from each wart, so we'll have six fire resistance potions in total."

"On the Xbox a fire resistance potion would give us three minutes of protection. Unless we had redstone, then they'd last for eight. I'm still not sure how time works in here. Still, even without adding redstone, three each should be enough."

"Three each? Are you the only one going across?" Jamie asked.

"Yes, no arguments," JJ said. "You've risked your life in the Nether, I won't let you risk it again." He held up his hands to stop Jamie from arguing. "Come on, we'll need to make an awkward potion before we can make the potion of fire resistance."

Jamie hesitated, then followed JJ's

instructions. He added three bottles of water to the bottom of the brewing stand.

"Okay, add the nether wart," JJ said when it began to bubble.

Jamie opened his inventory. The bubbles turned white when he added the nether wart, the brewing had begun. Thick smoke filled the air causing Annie to cough.

"Cover your mouth and nose." JJ put his blocky hands across his face indicating for the other two to do the same.

After a short time the nether wart disappeared.

"Good job, we've made an awkward potion," JJ said. "Now add the magma cream, it's the last step."

Jamie added the cream to the top box

in the brewing stand and they stood back as it boiled. Once again the room filled with smoke. As quickly as the room filled, it cleared again. The potion was finished.

JJ added the three bottles to his inventory. “Let’s make the other three.”

Jamie repeated the process. They covered their mouths and noses as the brewing stand bubbled and gurgled. It stopped and three new potions appeared.

JJ added the second lot of potions to his inventory and turned to his friends. “We’re ready. It’s time to rescue Charli.”

CHAPTER SIX

Unknown Hero

"Drink your three now," Annie said. "If it wears off halfway you won't burn up."

"It doesn't work like that," JJ said. "I have to drink one and when it begins to wear off drink the next one. If the lava starts feeling warm as I'm crossing I'll drink one straight away."

Annie's face was full of concern.

"I'll be fine," JJ said. "Three potions each will be more than enough. Come on, we need to free Charli before the professor comes back." JJ took one potion from his inventory and drank it.

There was no time to waste. He approached the lava with caution. He could still feel the heat but it was warm, not burning like before, the potion was working. He dipped a toe into the lake, still only warm. He jumped in and started to swim. He wondered if Charli could see him. He hoped so. The island was further than it looked and the lava was thick, much thicker than he'd expected.

JJ slowed down as his energy drained. He'd need to eat something to restore his hunger. He was only halfway across when the heat of the lava increased. The heat penetrated his skin. It began to burn. He accessed his inventory and drank another potion. The lava cooled. There were only four potions left. He had to reach Charli before drinking another. That would leave them with two each to return. Charli jumped up and down on the beach. Her excitement at seeing him made him move faster. He still had at least a minute before he would reach the island when the heat of the lava increased again. His heart sank as he drank a third potion.

"Are you okay?" Charli asked as JJ stepped onto the island.

"Yes, but we've got a problem. We made fire resistance potions but I used all three of my bottles to get here. I didn't think it would be so hard to swim across. I've got none left to get back." JJ took the remaining bottles from his inventory and threw them out in front of Charli. "These are for you. You'll need to drink one and when the lava heats up on the way back, drink another to cool yourself down."

"But what about you?"

"Tell Jamie he'll need to get more nether warts and make more potions. We'll have to hope the professor doesn't go mad when he finds me here instead of you. Quick, you need to go."

Charli hesitated.

"I mean it, go now."

She gave JJ a quick hug, drank one of the potions and jumped into the lava.

JJ watched as she swam back to Jamie and Annie. He couldn't believe it. All he'd done was swap places with Charli. He sat down. There had to be another way. He opened his inventory and chose some bread. He dug his feet into the sand and ate. There was one other way but did he have the guts to try it? He had an enderpearl. He could teleport with it. Was it possible to throw it to the other side of the lava lake? Was his throwing arm strong enough? He had full diamond armor so he wouldn't be badly hurt when he landed, unless he landed in the lava. He shivered. A fiery death would be horrible. There was no way to know what would happen if the professor returned. The enderpearl was his only chance of escape. Was it worth the risk?

Jamie and Annie rushed to hug Charli as

she exited the lava

"Where's JJ?" Jamie looked to the lake for his brother.

"He couldn't come. His potions ran out on the trip across. We're going to need to make more, a lot more," Charli said.

Jamie and Annie exchanged a look.

"What's wrong?" Charli asked. "We need to make them now."

"We don't have enough nether warts," Jamie said. "I'll need to go back to the Nether to get more."

Charli stared at Jamie. "You went to the Nether?"

Jamie nodded.

"Wow, now I'm glad I ended up on the island. I wouldn't have wanted to go to the Nether."

"Neither did I but it was the only way to make the potion."

A lump formed in Charli's throat. "You went there for me?"

Jamie punched her arm. "Of course I did you idiot. You would have done the same for me."

Charli wasn't so sure. The Nether terrified her.

"Okay, so how are we going to do this?" Annie asked.

"I'll go back in," Jamie said. "You and Charli hide while I'm gone. We can only hope the professor doesn't appear and work out what happened. If he takes his brewing stand or anything else with him we're in real trouble."

"Uh-oh, real trouble is approaching."

Annie grabbed Jamie and Charli and raced into the theme park. They hid behind the cake stall and peered through the cracks in its wooden walls. Annie was right. The professor had come back through the portal and now headed to his lab.

"I hope he doesn't realize we've used the brewing stand," Jamie said.

"He will," Annie said. "The room stank and we left the chests open."

They watched as the professor passed their hiding spot. An angry cry rose the moment he stepped into the lab.

Jamie stood. "Let's get out of here, he sounds furious. We don't want him to find us."

Charli and Annie followed as Jamie sprinted out of the theme park. Charli stopped, causing Annie to crash into her.

"What are you doing?" Annie said.

Charli pointed. "Something smashed into Jamie. It flew through the air and knocked him down."

Annie looked to see Jamie lying flat on his back. Someone else's legs lay across him, the rest of their body hidden by a grassy block. "Do you think it's the professor?"

Charli's lip quivered and she turned to Annie. "I'm too scared to look."

JJ groaned and rolled to his back. He hadn't landed in lava but whatever he hit was hard. A rock that moaned? He turned over and started to laugh. He couldn't help it. To throw an enderpearl far enough to save himself was awesome but to also hit his brother. Unbelievable. He looked up into the worried faces of Annie and Charli. He laughed even harder.

"Not funny," Jamie said. "That hurt."

"I know, I'm sorry, it's hard to believe it was even possible to hit you, that's all. Are you okay?"

Jamie pulled himself up and clambered to his feet. "I'm weak." He punched at his inventory pad. "My hunger's low. I need to restore it."

"I've got a better plan," Charli said. "The portal's only a short distance away. If we can get you there, we can go home."

"Great idea," JJ said. "Let's go before the professor finds us."

Annie and Charli each took one of Jamie's arms and led him to the portal. JJ followed. He wasn't hurt, the diamond armor had done its job. He smiled thinking again about his amazing throw.

"Something funny, is there boy?"

JJ clenched his fists and the smile disappeared from his face. This couldn't be happening, not now, not with the portal so close.

The professor laughed at the four Crafters' Club members. In his hands he held two large potions. "A special present for you," he said. "One drop of this and we'll get to test whether respawning is possible. One drop and you'll die."

Annie gasped, bringing the attention of the professor to her.

"Like to go first, would you?"

"No." JJ wouldn't let her be the first one to die in a map. He needed to protect her.

The professor laughed and turned to JJ. "Jealous are you? You can go first if you like. I don't mind who dies."

JJ wasn't given the opportunity to answer. The distant sound of hooves interrupted them.

"What's going on?" the professor said. "Friend of yours?"

The sound intensified as a horse appeared at the edge of the forest. It galloped toward the group. The rider's face was partially covered and he held a diamond sword.

Before JJ could yell to the others to

hide, the horseman swirled his sword and rode through the group. Dust filled the air between them and the professor. It was impossible to see him.

The horseman stopped and tipped his hat. "Enjoy your adventures, my friends." He put his hat back in place and nudged his horse into a gallop.

They watched as he rode off, disappearing around the side of a mountain.

"Guys," Charli said. "Guys, look what he did." The dust cleared revealing hundreds of inventory items. The professor was gone.

"Did he…did he kill him?" Annie's face was white.

JJ nodded. "He must have. The

inventory is all potions and other scientific things. This is the professor's inventory, I'm sure."

Annie looked as if she might cry.

JJ wrapped his arm around her. "It was him or us."

"I know but what if he died in the real world?"

"We'll never find out," JJ said. "We don't know who he was. Come on, let's go home, it's been a long day."

No one argued or suggested they explore further. The four members of the Crafter's Club linked arms and stepped into the purple light.

JJ glanced around as he landed on the soft

grass beside the portal. Annie, Charli, and Jamie stood next to him. He grinned, they were safe.

"Look," Jamie pointed to an empty soda can laying on the ground.

JJ walked over and picked it up. "I've never seen one like this." He held the can up for the others to see. It was blue and green with a jumble of letters that didn't make any sense.

Charli grabbed the can from him. "I have. The professor threw a potion on me from a can the same as this. He must have come through our portal."

"And brought something with him," Jamie said. "Maybe he brought the wolf-dog out too."

"The one we saw from the roller

coaster?" Charli asked.

JJ nodded. "Yes, we saw it in the real world. The question is whether it was a real dog he took in with him or one he brought out from the Minecraft map."

"So you can bring things out of the map?" Charli said.

"Maybe," JJ said. "The can and the dog suggest it's possible."

"At least we know he didn't die in the real world," Annie said. "What a relief."

"Is it?" Charli asked. "What if he comes after us?"

"How will he find us? We don't look like our Minecraft skins," Annie said. "Now come on, let's go back to JJ's and see if there's anything to eat. I don't know about you guys but I'm starving."

The four arrived at JJ's house delighted to find his mother making popcorn and brownies. She handed them a bowl of strawberries to add to their feast before she shut herself away in her office.

They took the food through to the family room. Minecraft music still played on the television.

"Thank goodness." Annie helped herself to a brownie. "I'm so hungry."

JJ took a handful of strawberries. "It's unbelievable. Think of everything we've been through and neither of my parents even think to ask what we're doing or where we've been."

Charli laughed. "They're happy we're

outdoors playing and they don't have to tell us to turn off the Xbox."

"These brownies are so good." Jamie licked the crumbs from his lips. "So who do you think the horseman was? He saved our lives. We should be doing something to thank him."

"Like what?" JJ asked.

"I don't know, maybe go in, talk to him, see if we can be useful." Jamie grabbed a handful of popcorn.

"We don't even know where to find him," JJ said.

"I saw horses from the roller coaster, they were near a waterfall," Charli said. "I know which direction to go."

"There's an easy way to find them," Jamie said. "We go back in on the Xbox and fly around in creative. We know which map he's in, once we find him we'll know exactly where to go when we go back through the portal."

JJ helped himself to a brownie. "You've got to be kidding. Do you honestly think any of us are going to go back through the portal after today? Charli was held prisoner, you risked your life in the Nether and the crazy professor tried to kill us. It was not a good day."

"Hold on, it was a great day," Jamie said. "You saved Charli, I didn't die in the Nether, and a masked hero killed the professor and saved all of us. It depends on how you look at it."

"Yeah, *and* you hit Jamie with an enderpearl and landed on him. Don't forget," Charli said with a grin.

"I'll never forget that. Hitting Jamie was the highlight for me."

"Don't be an idiot," Jamie said. "I'm serious. We should go back in and thank him. Riding a horse would be fun too." He waited for the others to agree, his face full of hope.

"There's no way. What if the professor's there?" JJ said.

"We'll make up a ton of potions before we go in," Jamie said. "Beat him at his own game. I doubt he'll risk going back after what the horseman did. And the dog wasn't a threat to us, he was friendly."

"Still, it's too dangerous. The girls agree with me, don't you?"

Annie and Charli glanced at each other.

"Well, you know I've always wanted to ride a horse," Annie said. "The professor has no reason to capture us again. If the soda can was his, he didn't die in the real world. That was the question he wanted answered."

"And it would be polite to say thank you to the horseman," Charli said.

JJ glanced from Jamie to the girls. Their eyes danced with excitment. He shook his head. "Please tell me you're kidding."

Books currently available in The Crafters' Club Series

Two Worlds
The Villagers
Lost
The Professor
Spirit
Friendship

Unforeseen problems destroy the thrill of locating the masked hero when the Crafters' Club members re-enter the Minecraft world. Frightening cave explorations, battles with mobs, and an intense rescue mission are some of the many challenges they face. Can the Crafters' Club piece together the clues required to help the hero, free a prisoner, and survive another exhilarating adventure?

Visit TheCraftersClub.com to purchase your copy of Spirit. Alternatively, chat with your favorite book retailer to order your copy.

Join The Crafters' Club – It's Free!

You too can join JJ, Jamie, Annie, and Charli as a member of The Crafters' Club. Prizes, special offers and advance notice of new book releases are just some of the benefits of belonging to the club. Sign up for free today at:

www.TheCraftersClub.com

Acknowledgments

Thank you to Ray and our two boys for their knowledge and instruction on all things Minecraft. Without your interest and enthusiasm The Crafters' Club would not exist. An extra thank you to Ray for your support, encouragement and input to the Crafters' Club series. Your website concept and design is outstanding.

A very special thank you to Minecraft fans and avid readers, Finn and Lyell, for their feedback on early drafts of the story. To Judy, a huge thank you for your well-utilized proofreading services.

Sincere thanks to Kathy Betts of Element Editing Services for your thorough editing and improvement of this story.

Finally, thanks to Lana Pecherczyk for her wonderful illustrations and cover design.

Made in the USA
San Bernardino, CA
20 March 2017